Where does Joe go?
Pearson, Tracey C   Test#: 34569
Points: 0.5   Lvl: 2.1

W9-DHJ-690

Lincoln School Library

T 8529

TRACEY CAMPBELL PEARSON

Where Does Joe Go?

A Sunburst Book · Farrar Straus Giroux

Copyright © 1999 by Tracey Campbell Pearson
All rights reserved

Distributed in Canada by Douglas & McIntyre Ltd.
Printed in Singapore
First edition, 1999
Sunburst edition, 2002
1 3 5 7 9 10 8 6 4 2

Library of Congress Cataloging-in-Publication Data
Pearson, Tracey Campbell.
    Where does Joe go? / Tracey Campbell Pearson. — 1st ed.
      p.   cm.
    Summary: Because Joe's Snack Bar always closes for the season,
the townspeople speculate about where Joe goes for the winter.
    ISBN 0-374-48366-3 (pbk.)
    [1. Fast food restaurants—Fiction.   2. Restaurants—Fiction.
3. Santa Claus—Fiction.]   I. Title.
PZ7.P323318Wh   1999
[E]—dc21
                                                    98-37745

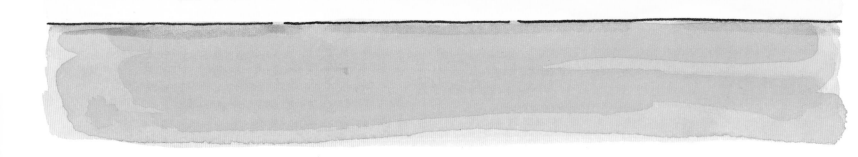

For Dennis

Every year, when winter is over and spring is finally here, Joe comes back to town.

Throughout the summer, crowds gather at Joe's

to eat hot dogs, creemees, and fries.

But after fall arrives, Joe disappears again, and

all winter long, everyone wonders: Where does Joe go?

"He's gone to the moon,"
cried tiny June.

"Or maybe the beach,"
said old Mr. Leach.

"I think he's on a cruise,"
said the woman buying shoes.

"He's having tea with the Queen,"
whispered Molly McLeen.

"He's digging for bones,"
said Oliver Jones.

"In Okefenokee!"
screamed Mrs. Bodoky.

"He's in the city,"
suggested Kitty.

"He's dancing the tango,"
said Mrs. Fandango.

"He's off to the pyramids,"
yelled all the Biddy kids.

"He's on a safari,"
said Charlie Maccari.

Then spring comes again, and the children call out,

"Joe, where have you been?"
But Joe won't tell a soul . . .

8385

E
PEA   Pearson, Tracey

           Where does Joe go?

DATE DUE		
NOV 1 5 2007		
2-5-08		
SEP 1 9 2008		
MAY 2 7 2008		
NOV 0 4 2008		
NOV 2 4 2009		
MAY 2 4 2011		

Lincoln School Library